GUINEA PIGS

Joanne Randolph

PowerKiDS
press™

New York

Published in 2007 by The Rosen Publishing Group, Inc.
29 East 21st Street, New York, NY 10010

First Edition

Editor: Joanne Randolph
Book Design: Julio Gil
Photo Researcher: Sam Cha

Photo Credits: All photos © www.shutterstock.com.

Library of Congress Cataloging-in-Publication Data

Randolph, Joanne.
   Guinea pigs / Joanne Randolph. — 1st ed.
      p. cm. — (Classroom pets)
   Includes index.
   ISBN-13: 978-1-4042-3676-9 (library binding)
   ISBN-10: 1-4042-3676-7 (library binding)
   1. Guinea pigs as pets—Juvenile literature. I. Title.
   SF459.G9R36 2007
   636.935'92—dc22
                                        2006026436

Manufactured in the United States of America

Contents

Picking a Guinea Pig for Your Classroom

Your class has decided to get a guinea pig! Have you thought about what kind of guinea pig you want? There are about 11 **breeds** in the United States. Guinea pigs are grouped based on how long their hair is and how the hair feels. They are also grouped by their color and markings.

Be sure that you pick a young animal that seems healthy. A healthy guinea pig has bright eyes and shiny, thick hair. It should have a dry nose and clean ears, too. Pick carefully! You do not want to take home a sick pet.

This long-haired guinea pig is called a Peruvian white. This kind of guinea pig will need to have its fur brushed and clipped.

Valued Pets

Guinea pigs are loving, friendly pets. In fact, these **rodents** have been valued as pets for thousands of years. The guinea pig, also known as the cavy, has lived in South and Central America for about 40 **million** years. It was **domesticated** and used as food as early as 9000 B.C.

The Europeans who sailed to the Americas starting in the 1400s brought these animals home to be kept as pets. They have been sitting on laps ever since!

Guinea pigs are nothing like pigs, and they are not from Guinea. People have been calling them by this name for hundreds of years, though.

One Guinea Pig or Two?

Guinea pigs are great pets for the classroom. They are **active** during the day and love lots of attention. Everyone will enjoy getting to know this new furry classmate.

In the wild, guinea pigs live in family groups of about five animals. This means that they like company. If you cannot spend a lot of time with your classroom pet, it might be a good idea to get two. Just be sure to give your pets plenty of space in their new home.

Males grow to be a bit larger and can be a bit more active than females. Some say females are more loving, though.

Home Sweet Home

Before your guinea pig comes into the classroom, you will need to get its home ready. Guinea pigs need space. One animal needs a cage that is at least 16 inches by 32 inches (41 x 81 cm). The bigger the cage, the happier your pet will be.

You also need to give the cavy a sleeping box or hiding place to make it feel safe. Give your pet lots of toys to climb on and chew, too. Guinea pigs' teeth are always growing. They need to chew to keep the teeth short.

You will want to have ripped-up paper or other bedding on the bottom of the cage. Topping this with hay or straw will make a nice, cozy home for your guinea pig.

Let's Eat

Your healthy guinea pig loves to eat! Be sure your pet gets lots of fresh, leafy, dark green vegetables, grass hay, and food **pellets**. Guinea pigs need a lot of vitamin C. This is why fresh greens are important. Some greens, such as spinach, beet tops, lettuce, and potato greens, can make your pet sick, though.

Your guinea pig's food should be placed in three different hoppers or in bowls. Do not forget to give your pet plenty of water, too.

Guinea pigs like kiwi fruit, oranges, peaches, apricots, grapes, apples, and strawberries. Be careful not to feed your pet too many fruits, though.

13

Picky Pigs!

Once your pet decides what foods it likes best, it may not want to eat anything else. Try not to change what you feed your guinea pig. If you do, your pet may decide not to eat at all. Guinea pigs have also been known to **starve** themselves because a new bowl was used for their food. Pick the easiest way for your class to feed your pet. Then stick with it!

If you need to change your pet's food, do it very slowly. This will help your picky pet make the change more easily.

Guinea pigs want their homes to stay just the way they are.
Changing its bowls and food can make your pet unhappy.

To Have and to Hold

Guinea pigs like nothing better than sitting in a person's lap. It is best to spend some time meeting the guinea pig while it is in its cage. You do not want to scare your new pet. After the cavy seems to know who you are, pick up the guinea pig carefully. Softly hold your pet so that it feels safe.

Guinea pigs can be badly hurt in even short falls. Hold the animal only if you are sure you will not drop it.

Pet the guinea pig softly. Guinea pigs let you know they are happy by purring and chattering their teeth.

Say What?

Guinea pigs talk to each other and to you in many ways. Two guinea pigs say hello by touching noses. A hopping, twisting, running guinea pig is playing. If your guinea pig is scared, it may run away. It also might stop moving at all.

Guinea pigs say hello to their owners by whistling. A whistle is a sound made by blowing air through the teeth. They chirp when they want help. They purr when they are happy. These are just a few of the ways your guinea pig talks to you every day!

Guinea pigs like to crowd together. If you have enough room for more than one, you can learn a lot about how these animals talk to each other.

A Healthy Pet

Taking care of your guinea pig is a big job. Everyone in your class needs to make sure your pet stays healthy and happy. The right care, food, water, and housing go a long way toward keeping your pet in good health.

What should you do if your guinea pig gets sick, though? As soon as you see signs that your pet is unwell, tell your teacher. He or she will need to bring your guinea pig to the **veterinarian** for a check-up.

You need to groom your guinea pig. This means taking care of its fur, teeth, and nails and checking its eyes and ears.

In the Classroom

Guinea pigs are great fun. It is your class's job to make sure your pet has the best life possible. If you are given a job to do, such as feeding the guinea pig or changing its water, do it. Your pet cannot live without you. Someone also must take care of the pet over long vacations and the summer. Are you ready to share your classroom with your new guinea pig?

Glossary

active (AK-tiv) Busy or moving.

breeds (BREEDZ) Groups of animals that look alike and have the same kin.

domesticated (duh-MES-tih-kayt-id) Raised to live with people.

million (MIL-yun) A very large number. One million is thousands of thousands.

pellets (PEH-lutz) Small, round things.

rodents (ROH-dents) Animals, such as mice, with long front teeth used for continuous chewing.

starve (STARV) To suffer or die from hunger.

vacations (vay-KAY-shunz) Trips taken for fun.

veterinarian (veh-tuh-ruh-NER-ee-un) A doctor who treats animals.

vitamin (VY-tuh-min) Something that helps the body fight illness and grow strong.

Index

B
bowl(s), 12, 14
breeds, 4

C
cage, 10, 16
cavy, 6, 10, 16
color, 4

D
day, 8

E
ears, 4
Europeans, 6
eyes, 4

F
food(s), 6, 12, 14, 20

G
green vegetables, 12

H
hair, 4
hay, 12
home, 8, 10

M
markings, 4

N
nose(s), 4, 18

R
rodents, 6

S
sleeping box, 10
space, 8, 10

T
teeth, 10
toys, 10

V
veterinarian, 20
vitamin C, 12

Web Sites

Due to the changing nature of Internet links, PowerKids Press has developed an online list of Web sites related to this book. This site is updated regularly. Please use this link to access the list:
www.powerkidslinks.com/cpets/gpigs/